THE PUDDLETO

Maggie Pearson lives in a
cottage in Suffolk. She has worked as a
librarian, barmaid, au pair, corn-dolly maker
and freelance journalist, but mostly as a
mother. Now that her three sons are grown
up, she is a full-time writer.

For my father, the best of storytellers

First published 1993 by Pan Macmillan Children's Books

a division of Pan Macmillan Publishers Limited
Cavaye Place London SW10 9PG
and Basingstoke

Associated companies throughout the world

ISBN 0 330 32584 1

Text copyright © 1993 Maggie Pearson
Illustrations copyright © 1993 John Eastwood

1 3 5 7 9 8 6 4 2

A CIP catalogue record for this book is available from
the British Library

Printed by Cox & Wyman Ltd, Reading, Berkshire

Maggie Pearson

THE PUDDLETOWN DRAGON

Illustrated by John Eastwood

**YOUNG
PIPER**

**Young Piper Original
PAN MACMILLAN
CHILDREN'S BOOKS**

CONTENTS

Chapter 1
FLYING NORTH

Every spring, the dragons fly north, to cool themselves in the arctic snows.

Some people will tell you that there are no dragons any more. "All killed off, they were," they say, "by knights in armour, rescuing fair maidens."

Some of them were. The stupid ones. The wise ones didn't sit about

waiting for a man in a tin suit to pick
a fight with them. They took
themselves off to the wild, lonely
places. To caves on the very tip-
tops of mountains, where you'd
need to sprout wings before you
could reach them. Or to the sandy
deserts, where a knight in his
armour would be frazzled to a crisp
by the sun before he came within
smelling distance of a dragon.

And when the desert gets too hot,
even for dragons, they fly north, led
by Great-grandmother Scorcher,
who is five hundred years old and
still growing.

One moonlit night, they flew over
Puddletown, a quiet sort of place,
where nothing ever happens. The
people there like it that way.

"Mama!" cried Smallest-of-all,
meaning, "My-wings-are-tired-and-
I'm-all-out-of-puff-and-I-can't-keep-
up-much-longer."

Mama was the only word he knew.
It made no difference anyway. None
of them heard him. The dragon fleet
sailed on, across the face of the
moon.

"Mama!" cried Smallest-of-all
again, as he tumbled, head over tail,

right out of the sky and into a field
of cows.

"Mama?" said Smallest-of-all.

The cows just stared, chewing the
cud and flicking their tails, the way
cows do, any hour of the day or
night.

"Mama!" sighed Smallest-of-all.
He picked himself up and set off
down the road towards the village.
Alice and her mother were just going
to bed when they heard a knock at
the door.

"Who can that be?" said Alice's mother. "At this time of night!"

"We'll never know unless we open the door," said Alice.

So she did. And Alice and her mother saw different things. Alice saw a small, green dragon, about knee-high to a girl of eight.

"Oh!" she said. "A dragon!"

Her mother saw the dragon's shadow thrown by the firelight on to the wall outside – and that shadow was huge!

"Oh!" she said. "A dragon!" She slammed the door and shot the bolt.

"Quick, Alice! Upstairs!"

"But, Mother—" said Alice.

"Don't be afraid, dear. I'll protect you."

"But, Mother—"

"We must warn the village!"

Alice had always thought it might be fun to tie the sheets together into

a rope and slide down from the back
bedroom window. She'd never
expected to see her mother doing it.
I suppose I'd better go too, thought
Alice: in case she hurts herself.

Chapter 2
PANIC IN PUDDLETOWN

Smallest-of-all, meanwhile,
wandered on, until he came to the
forge, where the blacksmith was
working late. The flames of the forge
threw strange shadows on the wall,
among them . . .

"A dragon!" yelled the blacksmith,
dropping the hammer on his foot.

Smallest-of-all watched, interested,
as the blacksmith hopped three
times round the anvil, holding his
toes.

"Mama?" asked Smallest-of-all.

But the blacksmith was off at a run
and already turning the corner at the
far end of the street. Smallest-of-all
walked on towards the centre of the
village and met the parson coming
out of church. The parson put down
his bicycle lamp while he locked the

door. He heard the shuffling of small feet behind him. He turned and took one look at the shadow on the wall.

Then he rushed back inside the church and began ringing the bells so hard that every back-swing lifted him clean off his feet.

The whole village came running. Some of them came to complain about the noise. Most of them came to see what the excitement was. The butcher. The baker. The Chair of the Parish Council, who was not a piece of furniture, but a lady wearing a flowery hat over her bedtime curlers.

Was it an accident? The doctor came, with his little black bag. Was it a fire? The Fire Brigade came, driving at top speed down the middle of the road. Was it murder, robbery and mayhem? The policeman came, with his truncheon at the ready. The landlord came from the village pub with a tray of drinks, because, whatever the excitement was, it was bound to make people thirsty.

The Oldest Inhabitant put on his
Home Guard helmet and came
marching down the road with a
pitchfork in his hand. They all
gathered in the church hall,
demanding to know what was going
on.

A dragon? A dragon! Huge, it was,
the parson told them. Breathing fire
and smoke, the blacksmith said.

"Green scales, great staring eyes
and roaring fit to wake the dead."
Alice's mother was not going to be
outdone.

"But, Mother—" said Alice.
"Hush, dear. The grown-ups are talking."

"There are no such things as dragons," the schoolmaster said.

"Perhaps you'd like to go and tell it so," Alice's mother suggested.

The schoolmaster said quickly that, whatever was out there, he thought it was the policeman's job to go and deal with it.

"Has it committed a crime?" the policeman asked.

"Not yet," said Alice's mother. "But it will do, if you don't go out there and arrest it."

"I can't arrest people for something they haven't done yet," said the policeman. "It wouldn't be fair." He thought the Fire Brigade should keep an eye on it, in case it set light to something.

It hadn't yet, the Fire Brigade said, and perhaps it wouldn't, but if they started following it about, it might, just to give them something to do. Perhaps it was a friendly sort of dragon, in which case, it was up to the Chair to say a few words of welcome.

But it seemed the Chair had left her welcome speech at home. Everyone thought someone else should be the one to face the dragon. So, in the end, nobody did. They talked till morning, drank all the beer and lemonade, then they all went home.

Chapter 3
PUDDLETOWN IS FAMOUS

But that wasn't the last of the story. Not by a long way. It was too good a story not to be told: how a dragon had appeared in Puddletown one dark night and kept the villagers prisoner in the church hall till morning.

They talked about it in shops and offices and pubs. In bus queues and on street corners. There was even a piece about it in the local paper.

Then reporters from the London papers, tired of being stuck indoors in this nice sunny weather having to write about boring things like Parliament, decided that the Puddletown dragon would make a good excuse for a few days in the country.

After them came the photographers.

The television cameras. And after
them, sightseers by the coach-load.
Nature lovers crouched in the fields,
binoculars at the ready.

The village shop was soon doing a roaring trade in marzipan dragons and had ordered a lorry-load of T-shirts with "I've been to see the Puddletown Dragon" written on the front. The village pub went to sleep one night under its old name, The Swan, and woke up next morning to find itself transformed into The Green Dragon.

The parson took visitors round the
church and showed them a carving
on the font which looked (very
nearly) like a dragon. All these years
he had thought it was meant to be a
dog. Or a deer. But he could see
now it was definitely meant to be a
dragon.

The Government sent in soldiers to protect the people. The Wildlife Protection people arrived to protect the dragon and every soldier found himself followed around by a figure in an anorak and green wellington boots. Some of them were so upset by it that they had to be sent home.

It was some time before anyone got round to asking the Big Question. The one that had been lurking at the back of their minds, only they'd all been too busy to put it into words.

"Where is this dragon, then?"

"I mean, it's supposed to be quite big, isn't it?" said the commander of the soldiers.

"Big as a house!"

"Bigger!"

"Breathing fire?" he asked. "That sort of thing?"

"Breathing fire – oh, yes!"

"Eyes like saucers, red and glowing!"

"Talons like – well, the sort of talons you'd expect on a dragon that size."

"What size?"

"Huge!"

"Bigger than that!"

"Gi-normous!"

Everyone in the village could describe the dragon by now, whether they'd seen it or not. The soldiers searched the fields, the empty barns, the woods and caves, with rifles at

the ready. The Wildlife Protection
people put down troughs of milk
and big platefuls of catfood and
went round calling: "Here! Draggie-
draggie-dragon!"

But not one trace of a dragon did
they find. Where was the dragon?
Well, to go back to that first
evening . . .

Chapter 4
HOW TO DEAL WITH DRAGONS

Smallest-of-all watched in some surprise as the villagers vanished one by one into the church hall and shut the door.

"Mama?" he said politely. Meaning, "It's-cold-out-here-and-lonely-so-may-I-come-in-please?"

Nobody heard him. He wandered away among the empty houses until he found himself back where he started, outside the house where Alice lived, with the rope of sheets still hanging down from the window. So up he climbed.

In the morning, Alice found him on her bed, curled up and fast asleep.

"Poor little thing!" she said.

Smallest-of-all opened one eye:

"Mama?"

Alice shook her head: "I'm not your mama."

But she did her best. Alice was a girl who liked looking after things. Her bedroom was a mess and her homework was never done in time and was always covered in blots and smudges. But when it came to animals, she somehow always managed to get things right. Little lost puppies turned up on her doorstep. Or a hedgehog, woken too soon from its winter sleep. Or a duckling with a broken leg.

There wasn't a bird for miles around that didn't know that Alice's garden was the place to go for a winter feed. Just as the owners of lost puppies usually knew that Alice's house was the first place to look.

The hedgehog she fed on scraps of meat, and clean water to drink. Then she found it a cool place at the back of the woodshed where it could sleep till spring came. She wrapped the duckling in a strong crepe bandage and wedged it between two

bricks so it couldn't move about
until its leg was healed. Faced with a
small dragon almost out of puff,
Alice knew exactly what to do.

First she fed him a little crumpled
paper. Then a few crispy, crunchy
twigs. Then bigger twigs. Then
small lumps of coal, until the fire
inside him was glowing nicely.

"Stay there," she said. "Don't go
away."

She took a bucket and went down
the road to the builder's yard.

"Please," said Alice, "could you
spare a bucket of sand?"

"Of course!" said the builder.
"What game are you playing now?"

"It's not a game," said Alice.

Back she went with her bucket of
sand and carried it up to her room.
And Smallest-of-all burrowed deep
inside it, tail first, until only the tip
of his nose was showing.

So Alice's mother never noticed him when she came in to make the bed each morning. If she noticed the bucket, it was no stranger than a lot of other things she'd found at one time or another in Alice's room: boxes of stones and jars full of leaves that generally turned out to be homes for caterpillars or frogs or

grass-snakes or some other sort of creeping, crawling thing. Alice's mother knew by now that the best thing was to leave them well alone.

If she noticed an odd smell of burning about the place from time to time, she put it down to one of the neighbours having a bonfire. Once she came in unexpectedly and found Smallest-of-all eating the buckles off Alice's best Sunday shoes. Smallest-of-all went rigid with fright while she picked him up and sat him on the end of the bed

between Fat Ted and Rupert
Rabbit.

But Alice's mother was much more
interested in the shoes than in
Alice's collection of soft toys. "Well,
look at that!" she exclaimed.
Smallest-of-all politely looked.

"She's lost the buckle off one of
her best Sunday shoes and never
told me. Now, where could that be,
I wonder?"

Smallest-of-all hiccupped: he'd
swallowed the buckle much too
quickly. It was nice, though.

By the time Alice came home, he'd
eaten the other buckle, the metal
buttons off her winter coat and the
ends of the zips on all her dresses.

Small bits of metal are like chocolate to a dragon: they can't get too much of them. Well, they can, but as soon as they feel better, they go off looking for more. Soon there wasn't a teaspoon or a thimble or a whole pair of scissors in the house.

Alice worried about this: she worried about him eating knives and she worried especially about pins. Every night she made sure her mother's pin cushion was locked away. She put a notice on her door *Please shut this door* but she couldn't be sure her mother would do it.

So every day she hurried home from school to see if Smallest-of-all was all right and kept an eye on him till bedtime.

"What are you doing up there?" her mother kept asking. "Why don't you go out and enjoy the sun?"

"I like it here," said Alice.

She didn't want to enjoy the sun. She much preferred the evening-time, just between light and dark, when she would open the window, and Smallest-of-all, after balancing a moment on the sill would spread his wings and fly free, looping and wheeling across the garden with shrill little cries, rather like a bat.

Look closely, next time you see
bats flying in the evening light: it's
just possible one of them might turn
out to be a very small dragon.
It's the tail that always gives them
away.

It was about this time that Alice
actually got top marks in school. It
was for an essay called "What I
know about Dragons". She seemed
to know so very much, she might
have got ten out of ten if she hadn't
been so careful to leave out any
mention of size. Instead she got nine
and a half.

Chapter 5
WANTED: ONE DRAGON

Sometimes Alice did wonder if she ought to tell someone about the dragon. But somehow the time never seemed to be quite right. If other people were talking about it, it was always, "Hush, child. Don't interrupt the grown-ups." If she tried to bring up the subject herself, it was, "There, there! Don't be frightened. Now I don't want to hear another word about that silly old dragon."

As the days went by it got harder. Each time the tale of the dragon was told, the dragon they thought they'd seen grew taller and fiercer. Each time Alice came home and looked again at Smallest-of-all, he looked more ridiculously small. What would people say when they found out the truth?

Probably not much: they'd be too busy laughing. Laughing at the people of Puddletown for making such a silly mistake. Laughing at Smallest-of-all, just for being small. Then they'd take him away and put him in a zoo in a great big cage all by himself, for people to stare at. "Call that a dragon?' they'd say. "But he's a wimp! He's a weed! He couldn't go three rounds with my granny!"

All things considered, there seemed to be just one thing to do. That was to do nothing. So that is what Alice did. With no fighting to do and no one to protect, the soldiers soon got bored and went away. The Wildlife Protection people heard of a panda that was having a hard time somewhere in China, so off *they* went.

The rest stayed on – and on – and on. Rather like the sort of relations who come for Christmas and are still hanging around come Easter-time. Always in the bathroom. Always wanting to watch the programme you *don't* want to watch on the telly.

The villagers kept saying things like, "Well, well! How time flies! I suppose you'll have to be going soon?" The reply was always the same: "Just as soon as we've seen the dragon."

Puddletown longed to be its old, quiet self again. Then, late one evening, the Chair had a brilliant idea. "They want to see a dragon, right?" she said. Everyone nodded. "And then they'll go away, right?"

"Right!" everyone agreed.

"Then we must show them a dragon. Simple!"

"Where are we going to get a dragon from?" the policeman asked.

"We can make one."

"How do you make a dragon?" asked the Fire Chief.

"The schoolmaster will know. He's always teaching the children how to make things out of washing-up liquid bottles and old lolly sticks and things like that."

They all went off to see the schoolmaster.

"We want you to show us how to make a dragon, please," they said.

"But that would be cheating!" the schoolmaster exclaimed, after they had explained their plan.

"Not really," said the Chair. "We all know we did have a dragon once. We've probably still got it somewhere about the place. We just can't put our hands on it at the moment. It does seem such a pity if all these people are going to be disappointed, after they've waited so long."

It would make a change, the schoolmaster thought, from papier mache piggy-banks and space rockets made from the inside of toilet rolls. He'd always wanted to work on something really big.

Chapter 6
THE HOME-MADE DRAGON

Next morning the green curtains had disappeared from the doctor's windows. The tea-shop was without its green-flowered tablecloths. Alice's mother packed up her green candlewick bedspread and carried it down to the church hall. The policeman's wife brought a ball-gown with five thousand sequins, all sewn on by hand, which looked as if it was going to leave an awkward glittery bit in the middle, until the landlord of the pub arrived with a box full of bottle-tops.

"What's going on?" asked one of the men from the papers, seeing the lights on in the church hall long after dark.

"Er – the Ladies' Sewing Circle. It's patchwork tonight. Do you want to come?"

"No, thank you."

It was patchwork, but patchwork
on a grand scale. Twice the length of
the hall, it was, when all the bits
were sewn together, and every shade
of green, as well as spots and stripes
and tartans, and studded with
bottle-tops that glittered red and
green and gold.

They stretched it over hoops made
from wire coat-hangers, then they all
climbed inside, with the

schoolmaster at the head. There was
no question at all that the
schoolmaster should be the one to
wear the head. He had made it. It
was knobbly with egg-boxes and
gleaming with milk-bottle tops and
hung with paper tassels that rustled
with the slightest movement. Its eyes
were like saucers, glowing red when
the schoolmaster switched on his
torch inside.

"What do you think?" they asked
the parson, who was the only one
left outside.

"Er," said the parson. He was a
truthful man and it reminded him
more than anything of the
caterpillars that kept eating his roses.
"Do you think it should have
wings?"

"Wings!" exclaimed the
schoolmaster. "Have you any idea
how big the wings would have to be
to lift a thing this size? They'd be

about as big as a football pitch!"

"I didn't mean you should make it fly. I meant, just for the look of it."

They found two old umbrellas and the Chair held them out, one on each side. The parson said that looked much better. At least it took his mind off all those feet.

Just as the sun was rising the dragon set off up the hill, while the parson went to ring the church bells, as he'd done before. People woke up. The men from the papers and the television, and the nature lovers, who never slept much anyway, since they would stay out in the fields, no matter what the weather.

None of them noticed that the Puddletown people didn't seem to have been woken by the noise. They were too busy watching the Puddletown dragon as it climbed slowly up the hill.

Chapter 7
TOO MANY DRAGONS

It was a splendid sight. The early
morning mist hid all the little legs
and the rising sun gleamed on the
bottle-tops. Now and again the
dragon turned its head, so that they
could see the glaring of its eyes.

The visitors watched until it was
out of sight, then they went inside to
pack their things. So there was no
one to see the Puddletown dragon
appear again on top of the hill,
running backwards towards the
village with a sort of concertina
movement, as those people nearest

the head tried to overtake those
nearer the tail. Bottle-tops flew in all
directions. Bits of material caught
on bushes that seemed to have
sprung up in the last ten minutes,
just to get in the way. The Chair,
still with an umbrella in each hand,
found herself hang-gliding for the
first and last time in her life. It was
the schoolmaster who reached the
village first, though he'd had the

furthest to run. Coming face to face with Great-grandmother Scorcher on the far side of the hill had given him the turn of speed that wins Olympic medals.

"The dragon!" he panted, pointing up the hill.

"Yes, thank you very much. We've seen the dragon."

"I mean a real, live dragon. Big as a house! Eyes like saucers! Breathing fire! Talons like, like . . ."

"That's the one. Don't worry. It seems quite harmless."

"Harmless?" squeaked the schoolmaster. "Harmless! You haven't seen it!"

"Yes we have. We've got our pictures. Goodbye!"

The reporters, photographers and sightseers climbed into their cars and vans and on to their bicycles and then they were gone, leaving

Puddletown with a real, live dragon on its doorstep.

Great-grandmother Scorcher settled down, with her chin resting on top of the hill.

The villagers bolted their doors and drew the curtains. Not that that would have done much good against a determined dragon who wanted to come in.

Night fell. Nobody slept.

Great-grandmother Scorcher's breath was a fiery column in the sky, reflecting the red glow of her eyes. Morning came and the villagers crept out of their houses, counted themselves and felt a lot braver when they'd made sure nobody had been eaten.

"What does it want?" they wondered. "Sitting there! It must have a reason. What does it want?"

"It's not an it," said Alice. "It's a she.

I know what she wants."

She began to walk up the hill.

"But, Alice—" said her mother.

"Hush, Mother," said Alice.
"Don't be afraid."

"But, Alice . . . What's that you're
carrying?"

"A dragon," said Alice. "They
come in all sizes."

Nobody laughed at Smallest-of-all.

They said, "Ah!" and "Isn't he sweet!" and "Can I hold him?"

Alice just walked on until she reached the top of the hill and there she put him down.

"Mama," said Smallest-of-all, meaning, "I-didn't-mean-to-get-left-behind-and-I'm-sorry."

Great-grandmother Scorcher understood. When you're five hundred years old, you get to understand things without being told properly. She stretched out a wing for him to climb up.

Smallest-of-all settled himself on top of her head and took a firm grip on her horns. Then he looked down at Alice.

"Alice," he said.

Alice knew exactly what he meant. He meant, "Goodbye-Alice-and-thank-you-for-looking-after-me."

Great-grandmother Scorcher
purred with a sound like the rumble
of a steamship's engine. It's a big
day for dragons when baby learns a
new word. Proudly she spread her
wings and turned her head towards
the north.

It would have made a splendid picture for the television cameras, Alice watching them fly out of sight. It would have been a wonderful story for the papers. A story to be told over and over on street corners and at bus stops and in shops and pubs and offices. But it never was. Because Puddletown is a quiet sort of place. The people there like it that way.

57

All Pan books are available at your local bookshop or newsagent, or can be ordered direct from the publisher. Indicate the number of copies required and fill in the form below.

Send to: Pan C. S. Dept
             Macmillan Distribution Ltd
             Houndmills Basingstoke RG21 2XS
or phone: 0256 29242, quoting title, author and Credit Card number.

Please enclose a remittance* to the value of the cover price plus: £1.00 for the first book plus 50p per copy for each additional book ordered.

*Payment may be made in sterling by UK personal cheque, postal order, sterling draft or international money order, made payable to Pan Books Ltd.

Alternatively by Barclaycard/Access/Amex/Diners

Card No. ⬚⬚⬚⬚⬚⬚⬚⬚⬚⬚⬚⬚⬚⬚⬚⬚⬚⬚

Expiry Date ⬚⬚⬚⬚⬚

Signature:

Applicable only in the UK and BFPO addresses

While every effort is made to keep prices low, it is sometimes necessary to increase prices at short notice. Pan Books reserve the right to show on covers and charge new retail prices which may differ from those advertised in the text or elsewhere.

NAME AND ADDRESS IN BLOCK LETTERS PLEASE:

....

Name_____

Address_____

_____

_____

_____

6/92